This book belongs to:

_____

A catalogue record for this book is available
from the British Library

Published by Ladybird Books Ltd
A subsidiary of the Penguin Group
A Pearson Company
© LADYBIRD BOOKS LTD MCMXCVIII

LADYBIRD and the device of a Ladybird are trademarks of
Ladybird Books Ltd Loughborough Leicestershire UK

How could you, Jepp?

written by Elizabeth Dale

illustrated by David Kearney

One morning, as Jenny and her family were eating breakfast, Mr Walsh came rushing into the kitchen. He looked worried. As a vet with a busy practice his day often started early and it seemed to be one of those days. He had his black medicine bag in one hand.

"I've just had a phone call from Bill Giles. Something's been attacking his lambs," he said.

"Oh, no!" cried Jenny's sister Caroline. She and Jenny had seen Mr Giles' lambs being born.

"What did it?" asked Matthew, Jenny's brother.

"A dog," said her dad.

"Wuff!" barked Jepp, their collie, lifting up his ears.

"Not you, old fella!" laughed Mr Walsh, stroking him. "Hey, you're wet!"

"He's just come back from a long run," said Mrs Walsh. "He got out through the hole in the fence again."

"There's blood on his nose," said Mr Walsh.

"Oh, Jepp!" said Mrs Walsh, her hands on her hips. "You haven't been sniffing around Johnson's again, have you?"

Jepp hung his head and the children laughed. There was no place Jepp liked better than Johnson's, the village butcher. Fortunately, Mr Johnson liked Jepp and often gave him titbits to eat.

"How could anyone have a dog that killed sheep?" asked Caroline, when her dad had gone.

"They don't know that their dog is killing them," said her mum. "Some dogs go wild when they're near sheep. But they're perfectly tame the rest of the time. They're called sheep-worriers."

The children were just leaving for school when Mr Walsh got back. He had a tiny lamb in his arms.

"Aah!" cried Jenny when she saw him. "He's sweet!"

"He's badly hurt," said Mr Walsh. "I need to operate on him."

Straight after school, Jenny brought Tom, her best friend, home to see the little lamb. He was lying in a box surrounded by straw, but already he looked stronger.

"He's so cute," said Jenny, stroking him. "Is he getting better?"

"Yes," said Mr Walsh, "he's almost well again. But unfortunately he's an orphan now. His mother was attacked by the sheep-worrier, too."

"Can we feed him?" asked Tom.

"Of course," said Jenny's dad. "I'll get a bottle."

Just then the phone rang.
Mrs Walsh popped her head
round the door.

"It's Frank Smith," she said.
"Something's been attacking his
    sheep now!"

        "Oh, dear!" cried Jenny.

"That's not all," said Mrs Walsh. "I think you'd better come and talk to him."

Jenny and Tom stroked the lamb while Mr Walsh answered the phone. And then he rushed out without even saying 'goodbye'!

"What's the matter?" Jenny asked her mum.

"Nothing," she said. But she looked worried. Something was wrong. Why wouldn't she tell them?

"When Jepp comes back, will you tell me?" her mum asked.

Jenny suddenly felt terribly afraid.

"The sheep-worrier hasn't attacked Jepp, too, has he?" she asked.

"No, of course not!" said her mum. "Whatever gave you that idea?"

But Jenny couldn't help worrying. She and Tom went to look for Jepp, and when he came running back into the yard, they ran to greet him.

"You're all right!" Jenny said, hugging him.

"See, Jepp's fine!" Jenny said, taking him inside, but her mum didn't smile. Instead, she examined him closely.

"What's the matter?" asked Jenny.

"Jepp shouldn't keep getting out," said her mum. "I know he only runs over the fields, but he must stay inside from now on."

When Mr Walsh came home, he didn't look any happier.

"One sheep killed," he said, "and three injured."

And then he and Mrs Walsh went into the lounge, shut the door and started whispering.

Just then there was a loud knock on the door. Jenny answered it.

It was Mr King, their neighbour, but he wasn't smiling as he usually did.

"I need to see your dad," he told Jenny. "Urgently!"

Mr King joined Jenny's mum and
dad in the lounge. Jenny and Tom
could hear him talking angrily.

When Mr King finally left, Mr Walsh called Jenny into the lounge. He put his arm round her.

"I've got something very sad to tell you," he said. "It seems that Jepp is the one who's been attacking the sheep."

"No!" cried Jenny, so loudly that Caroline and Matthew came rushing to see what was wrong.

Mr Walsh explained to them all how
Mr Smith and Mr King had both
seen Jepp with the sheep when
they'd been attacked.

"And he did come home with blood
on his nose this morning,"
said Mrs Walsh.

"It wasn't Jepp, it can't have been!" cried Jenny.

She ran to Jepp and flung her arms round his neck.

"He's too gentle! He'd never hurt anything!" she said. And Tom, Caroline and Matthew all agreed with her.

"They all saw him," said Mr Walsh.

"It must be a dog that looks like him!" cried Matthew.

"No," said Mrs Walsh, quietly. "There was blood on his mouth again tonight."

"As a vet I have to set an example to other dog-owners," said Mr Walsh. "He'll have to be put down."

"No!" cried Jenny. She ran up to her room and flung herself on her bed. She couldn't bear it if Jepp died.

Her mum and dad came to talk to her, but Jenny couldn't be consoled. She knew that Jepp wouldn't harm any sheep – she had to save him!

The next morning, Jenny got up early and went to see Jepp. Sensing something was wrong, he didn't bound over to greet her as usual.

"Can we take him for a walk before breakfast?" she asked her dad. "Please? He deserves one last walk."

"All right," said Mr Walsh. "But he must stay on a lead."

It was a beautiful day. Once he was outside, Jepp brightened up. He pulled on the lead and Jenny ran with him, leaving her dad behind. As soon as they were far enough ahead, she slipped the lead off him.

"Go on, Jepp!" she cried.

Jepp turned and looked at her with a puzzled look on his face.

"Go!" Jenny cried. "Run! Run as fast as you can and don't come back!"

Jepp stared at her with his big brown eyes.

"Oh, go, Jepp, you stupid dog!" shouted Jenny, tears streaming down her face. "Don't you see, I'm trying to save you! Run!"

Just for a moment, Jepp stood there.
And then he ran. Jenny flopped
down on the ground, crying.
She'd done it!

"Jenny!" cried her dad, running up.
"What's the matter? Did you fall?
Stop crying and tell me
what happened."

But Jenny couldn't stop. Jepp had gone. And then she heard a terrible noise. The sheep in the next field were all bleating very loudly. Mr Walsh and Jenny both looked over the hedge in alarm. The sheep were racing all over the field and there running after them was a black and white dog – Jepp!

Jenny couldn't believe it! Jepp was the sheep-worrier! And now, because of her, he was chasing more sheep.

"Look!" cried her dad, pointing.

Jenny didn't want to look, but she forced herself to. Suddenly she realised what was really happening.

Jepp wasn't chasing the sheep at all. He was chasing another dog – the large, black dog who had been attacking the sheep. Jepp was saving the sheep!

"Go on, Jepp!" she shouted. And Jepp did. He chased the black dog until it was out of sight.

"You clever dog!" cried Jenny as Jepp bounded up to her.

"He certainly is!" said Mr Walsh. "Hey, what's this?"

He frowned as Jepp licked a wound on his leg. "That's not new!" he said, examining it. "So that's why you had blood on your nose yesterday afternoon!"

"And you really had been to Johnson's in the morning!" laughed Jenny. She hugged Jepp. "I never doubted you, Jepp. I knew you weren't bad. I do love you!"

And Jepp gazed at her out of his big, brown eyes, as though to say he loved her, too.

Mr Walsh tells you more about… an animal hospital

Animal hospitals like Greenbanks are well equipped to care for sick animals. Each hospital has specially trained staff who know exactly how to make sick or injured animals better. A hospital will also have an X-ray machine, to check for broken bones, and an operating theatre.

No animal is turned away from Greenbanks unless it's too large. We are especially pleased to help wild animals. I feel we are particularly responsible for them as nearly all wild animal injuries are caused by humans, especially their cars.

Meet the characters…

Mr Walsh
a vet

Mrs Walsh
a veterinary nurse

Jenny Walsh
nine years old